Fergal's Flippers

Illustrated by DAVID MELLING

LUCY DANIELS

Hodder Children's Books

A division of Hodder Headline Limited

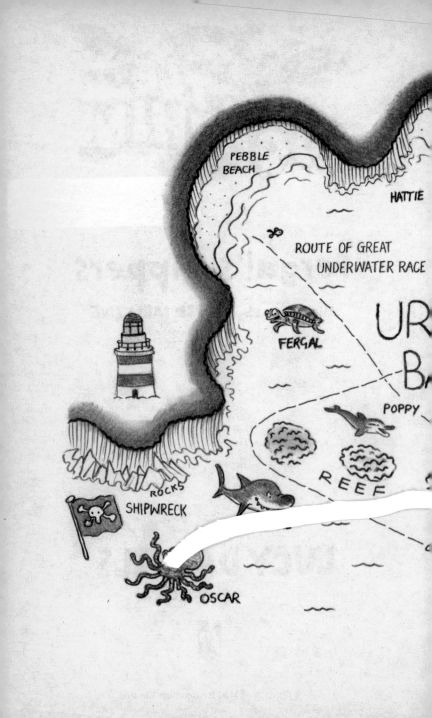

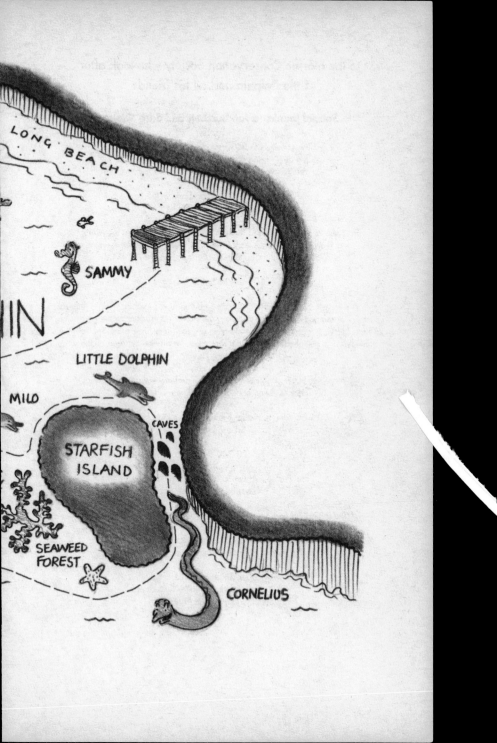

To the Marine Conservation Society who look after Little Dolphin and all his friends

Special thanks to Jan Burchett and Sara Vogler

Text copyright © 2005 Working Partners Limited
Created by Working Partners Limited, London, W6 0QT
Illustrations copyright © 2005 David Melling

First published in Great Britain in 2005
by Hodder Children's Books

10 9 8 7 6 5 4 3 2 1

A Catalogue record for this book is available from the
British Library

ISBN 0 340 87350 7

Printed and bound in Great Britain by
Clays Ltd, St Ives plc

The paper and board used in this paperback by Hodder Children's
Books are natural recyclable products made from wood grown in
sustainable forests. The manufacturing processes conform to the
environmental regulations of the country of origin.

Hodder Children's Books
A division of Hodder Headline Limited
338 Euston Road, London NW1 3BH

CHAPTER ONE

It was the day before the Great Underwater Race in Urchin Bay. Little Dolphin, Milo and Poppy were very excited. For the first time, they were being allowed to take part! The race was a long one – even for grown-ups – so Captain Capes, the chief race organizer, had said they should swim as a relay team.

"I can't wait for tomorrow!" Little Dolphin chirped, as they watched the other competitors practising in the sparkling blue water.

For as long as he could remember, Little Dolphin had watched the famous race and cheered as the contestants sped round Urchin Bay to the finishing line at Pebble Beach. Taking part was a dream come true!

"Uh-oh!" said Poppy suddenly. "Here comes our coach and her assistants. Quick, pretend we're warming up."

They began to waggle their

flippers as Hattie the hermit crab scuttled towards them. Oscar the octopus and Fergal the turtle were close behind.

Hattie took her job as coach very seriously. She clicked her pincers for attention. "Let's run through our plan for tomorrow, team," she said.

"I start the race at the jetty," chirped Poppy, spinning with excitement. "And I zoom along the coral reef till I get to Milo at Lighthouse Rock."

"And what do you do then, Milo?" asked Hattie.

"Don't remember," said Milo. He was gazing at Karen the killer whale who flashed past,

blowing a huge waterspout as she rose to the surface.

Little Dolphin grinned. Milo was a terrible scatterbrain!

"Poppy taps your flipper and you take over," snapped Hattie, whiskers twitching.

"That's right!" exclaimed Milo cheerfully. "And I speed round Starfish Island until I get to Little Dolphin at the seaweed banks."

"Then I head for Pebble Beach," Little Dolphin carried on. "And the end of the race!"

"And we'll all be cheering loudly!" declared Oscar, wiggling his arms into a tangle.

"I might wave – if there aren't too many people watching," whispered Fergal, who was very shy.

"Are you sure you don't want to be in the race, Fergal?" Little Dolphin asked. "You're such a good swimmer."

But the thought sent Fergal

 disappearing inside his shell.

"We'll practise the bit where Milo takes over from Poppy," said Hattie. "Poppy, you swim up to Milo. And Milo, don't shoot off before Poppy's touched your flipper this time. Remember the rules – you must touch flippers or it's cheating. Fergal, make sure they do it right."

Little Dolphin stood on his tail in the sand next to Milo. "I'll pretend to be Lighthouse Rock," he chirped.

Poppy set off towards Milo, spinning as she went. But when she reached him she whacked his flipper so hard that he spun into Little Dolphin and knocked him sideways into a seaweed bush!

"Hope you don't do that to the real lighthouse!" chuckled Oscar.

"It's no laughing matter, Oscar!" Hattie told him. "Check Little Dolphin for injuries. He's got to be fit for tomorrow!"

At that moment the water around them churned and something swished by at high speed.

"Look at Hamish!" exclaimed Oscar.

"He's so fast!" sighed Poppy as they watched Hamish the hammerhead shark disappear into the distance with powerful lashes of his tail.

"We'd need three tails each to swim that quickly!" Little Dolphin grinned.

"You'll have to manage with the ones you've got," said Hattie briskly. "Lunchtime now. We'll practise again this afternoon at the old wreck."

The three dolphin friends said goodbye to Hattie, Fergal and Oscar, and set off for their homes. They dodged a shoal of lemon tang fish who were racing each other round the reef. It seemed as if everyone in Urchin Bay was practising for the race.

Even Mrs Slither the sea snail was doing her usual speed trial along the sand. Mrs Slither always took part in the Great Underwater Race, although by the time she'd finished everyone else had forgotten about it!

Then they saw a familiar grey shape swimming towards them.

"Look out!" said Milo. "It's Vinnie!"

"That shifty shark is sure to try and sell us something we don't want," Little Dolphin clicked.

But Vinnie swam past them as if they weren't there! He didn't even give his usual toothy grin.

"That's strange!" Little Dolphin said, puzzled. "There must be something wrong with him."

"Up to no good, more likely," snorted Milo.

"Let's find out!" said Poppy, who was very nosy.

Keeping their distance, they followed Vinnie round the reef.

Suddenly, another shark popped up out of a bed of long eelgrass to meet him. The sharks looked just like each other!

The three friends ducked out of sight behind a rock.

"Which one's Vinnie?" Milo asked, looking confused.

The shark in the eelgrass gave a big toothy grin.

"That's Vinnie," said Poppy. "I'd know those teeth anywhere."

"Then the other one must be his twin brother!" Little Dolphin replied.

"Vernon, my man!" called Vinnie. "I've been waiting ages for you!"

"It's a long way from Shady Cove," said Vernon, sinking down on to the sand. "I'm tired out!"

"Lazy, more like," said Vinnie scornfully. "Shady Cove's only just beyond the headland."

Vernon grunted. "What d'you want me for anyway?"

"You're going to help me win the Great Underwater Race!" Vinnie told him.

"But I've never swum a race in my life," spluttered Vernon.

"You won't have to," smiled Vinnie, looking round shiftily. "We're going to cheat!"

CHAPTER TWO

Little Dolphin, Milo and Poppy looked at each other in astonishment.

"They're going to cheat!" clicked Poppy.

"Maybe it's just a joke," Little Dolphin said. "We'd better find out."

"The Great Underwater race has a really cool trophy,"

they heard Vinnie tell his twin
brother. "White rock with pearls
all over it. When we win it I'll
put it by my cave and everyone
will stop to admire it. Then I'll
get them talking, and before
you know it they'll be buying
everything I show them! It will
be great for business!"

"Wait a minute!" said Vernon.
"That trophy sounds just what *I*
need. I've always wanted to join
the Shady Cove Supersharks –
they have such brilliant parties.
Trouble is, you're supposed
to have won medals and
things, and that's just too tiring.

But they'll let me join if I have the Great Underwater Race trophy!"

"No, it's *my* plan," snapped Vinnie. "*I'm* having it."

"Then I'm not helping!" snarled Vernon.

The two sharks glared at each other, teeth glinting.

Then Vinnie grinned craftily.

"Silly to argue," he said. "We'll share the trophy. I'll have it first, then you keep it for a while. Now, do you want to know my plan or not?"

"All right," agreed Vernon.

"I'll draw it for you," said Vinnie.

Little Dolphin peeped round the rock to get a good look. He watched as Vinnie drew a wobbly circle in the sand with his snout.

"Imagine this is Urchin Bay," Vinnie said. He added a crooked line. "This is the jetty where the race starts. I'll zoom off with all the others until I reach here." He drew a blob. "That's the coral reef. Now, the really clever bit's coming up so you'd better be listening."

"'Course I am!" grunted Vernon.

"Good," said Vinnie. "When I reach the reef I hide in a cave!"

"What d'you want to do that for?" spluttered Vernon.

"Because, you overgrown sardine, I'm not fast enough to win on my own," snarled Vinnie. "That's why I need *you*. You'll be hiding in the seaweed banks right over here." He added some squiggles to his diagram. "That's nearly the end of the race. The moment you see the leaders coming in the distance, you set off in front of them – and win! The trophy will be mine ... I mean, ours. What d'you think?"

Vernon nosed at the map. "You're hopeless at drawing," he said at last.

"Never mind the drawing, seaweed brain!" cried Vinnie.

"What do you think of my plan? Brilliant, isn't it! And, as no one knows I've got a twin brother, no one can possibly find out what we've done!"

"I won't have to swim too far, will I?" asked Vernon doubtfully.

"Couple of tail flaps!" Vinnie assured him with a sly smile.

"And we share the trophy?"

"Er ... yeah, of course!"

"Then I'll do it!" exclaimed Vernon.

"That's my boy!" beamed Vinnie. "Can't wait to hold that trophy in my flippers!"

Vernon scowled at him.

"I mean, *our* flippers," Vinnie said hurriedly. He gave Vernon a whack with his tail. "You scarper off back to Shady Cove until tomorrow. We don't want anyone seeing us together before the race, now do we?"

Little Dolphin drew his head back and turned to his friends. "Those two crafty sharks really are going to cheat!" he clicked anxiously. "And we've got to do something about it!"

CHAPTER THREE

After lunch, Little Dolphin, Milo and Poppy met Hattie, Oscar and Fergal by the old wrecked ship. But there was no time for training. They were too busy telling their news.

Hattie was very angry when she heard about Vinnie's shifty plan. "I'm going to report them to Captain Capes!" she said crossly.

And she began to strut off, whiskers waving furiously.

"Wait, Hattie," Little Dolphin whistled. "We can't prove anything. Vinnie will pretend we've made it up!"

Hattie stopped. "I suppose you're right," she clicked grumpily.

"I've an idea," said Fergal shyly. "Don't tell Captain Capes … let Vinnie and Vernon try to cheat and—"

"That's not a plan at all!" snorted Hattie.

The turtle was so upset he disappeared inside his shell.

"I don't think Fergal's finished, Hattie," Little Dolphin told her.

"Sorry," said Hattie, "but those shifty sharks have made me hopping mad!"

"Come on, Fergal," chirped Poppy, trying to peer inside his shell. "Tell us your plan."

"Let them try to cheat," came a small voice, "but make sure it doesn't work." Fergal's head emerged slowly. "Teach them a lesson," he nodded.

"That's a great idea!" Little Dolphin whistled.

Fergal turned pink with embarrassment.

"So how do we stop Vernon getting to the finishing line first?" asked Poppy.

"Tie him up?" grinned Oscar, wrapping his arms into knots.

"Or move the sign that points to the finish?" suggested Milo.

"Then *everyone* will get lost!" snorted Hattie.

All of a sudden something stirred in the darkness of the old wreck. A strange pale shape loomed up from a battered

porthole.
It was
coming
straight for
them! Forgetting
their plans, they all
dived for cover.

"It's a ghost!" Milo
squeaked in fright. "Hide,
everybody!" He buried his head
in the sand.

Fergal disappeared inside his
shell again, and Little Dolphin,
Poppy and Oscar shot off in
opposite directions.

Hattie was rooted to the
spot with fright. Her eyes stood

out on their stalks as the spooky shape floated overhead. And then she burst out laughing. "Come back, everyone!" she chuckled. "There's nothing to be scared of!"

Milo pulled his head out of the sand. "Has the ghost gone?" he asked.

"It wasn't a ghost at all," snorted Hattie, as Little Dolphin, Poppy and Oscar swam anxiously back. "It was a jellyfish!"

"If it was only a jellyfish," quavered Poppy, "what's making that rattling noise?"

"That's Fergal!" said Hattie, pointing a claw at the terrified turtle.

Fergal was shivering so much his shell was knocking against the side of the wooden wreck.

"It's all right, Fergal," Little Dolphin called. He swam over and gave Fergal's shell a gentle nudge. "You can come out now. There's nothing to be scared of."

Fergal's head appeared.

"Silly me," he said, going pink again.

"You're not silly!" Milo chirped. "We were all frightened. I bet even the biggest whale in the ocean would have thought that jellyfish was a ghost!"

"That's given me an idea!" Little Dolphin said suddenly. "I know what we can do to stop Vinnie and Vernon cheating!"

CHAPTER FOUR

"We'll make *Vernon* think he's
seen a ghost too!" Little Dolphin
chirped. "He'll be too scared to
come out of the seaweed banks!"

"And he won't finish the
race!" exclaimed Hattie.

"But where are we going to
find a ghost?" asked Milo.

"I'm not going on a ghost
hunt!" clicked Poppy anxiously.

"It doesn't have to be a real ghost," Little Dolphin told them. "One of us could dress up." He looked around – and spotted a tattered white sail that still hung from the rigging of the old wrecked ship. "And I know just what we could use!"

He swam over to the sail, tugged it free with his teeth and

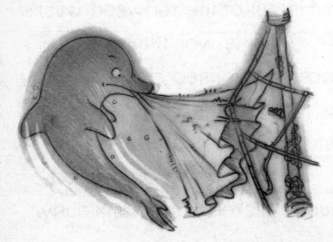

pulled it back to his friends. "Who wants to try being a scary ghost?" he chirped.

"Me!" squeaked Poppy, diving under the sail. But in her excitement, she started to spin. Before her friends could stop her she'd wound herself up so tightly she looked like a big white water worm floundering in the sand.

"That won't scare Vernon!" chuckled Oscar as he untangled Poppy from the sail. "He'll just laugh his flippers off!"

"You can't be the ghost anyway, Poppy," said Hattie firmly. "Nor can Little Dolphin or Milo. You'll all be racing. I'll do it – prepare to be terrified!"

Hattie crawled under the sail.

There was a muffled 'Wooo!' from underneath and she scuttled back out. "What do you think of that?" she said proudly.

"You wouldn't have scared a passing pilchard!" grinned Milo.

Hattie's whiskers bristled and she snapped her claws crossly.

"You'd make a wonderful ghost, Hattie!" Little Dolphin chirped quickly, before Milo got nipped. "But we need our trainer to be at the finishing line."

Hattie pulled in her claws. "Of course!" she said importantly. "But who's left? Oscar could never keep the sail on over all those legs."

Oh dear, Little Dolphin thought. Perhaps his idea wasn't such a good one after all.

Suddenly the sail began to flutter as if it was alive! It rose up until it towered above Little Dolphin and his friends.

They huddled together in a shivering bunch. Could it be a real ghost this time?

Then the sail sunk slowly down on to the sea-bed – and out crawled Fergal! "Don't suppose that was scary," he said shyly.

"It was terrifying!" exclaimed Milo.

"How did you get the sail to move in such a spooky way?" asked Poppy shakily.

"Easy!" Fergal told them. "Just flapped my flippers!"

"That's it!" Little Dolphin whistled. "You need turtle flippers

to be a really good ghost. Fergal will be our ghost tomorrow!"

"One problem," mumbled Fergal. "Too scared on my own."

"Don't worry. I'll be there," Little Dolphin told him. "The seaweed banks are where I take over from Milo in the race."

"One more problem," muttered Fergal doubtfully. "Too scared to say, 'Wooo'."

"Don't worry about that," said Oscar. He scooped up a large conch shell from the sea-bed. "Have another go, Fergal. This time with sound effects!"

Fergal disappeared under the sail. Oscar put the shell to his mouth. Suddenly all around them was a loud spooky wailing and the sail rose and started to quiver. It looked more ghostly than ever!

"Are you sure that's Fergal?" quavered Milo. He risked a peep under the sail. "It's OK, everyone – it *is* him."

Fergal slipped the sail off.

"Brilliant!" said Hattie. "It sent shivers up my whiskers when you started to shake."

"Didn't mean to shake," said Fergal faintly. "It was that awful noise. Frightened me!"

"If you can get those flippers quivering tomorrow," Little Dolphin chirped, "you'll terrify Vernon."

"No problem," said Fergal. "I'll be terrified too."

CHAPTER FIVE

Everyone in Urchin Bay had turned out to watch the Great Underwater Race.

Little Dolphin, Oscar and Fergal dashed over to the other side of the bay, far away from the cheering crowds. When they got close to the seaweed banks, they could see Vernon skulking in the darkness, ready to sneak into the lead.

They quickly hid behind the big waving leaves of a kelp bush.

"Everyone ready?" Little Dolphin asked his friends in a whisper.

Oscar grinned and held up the conch shell.

"Think so," quavered Fergal from underneath his sail.

All of a sudden they heard distant cheering from Starfish Island.

"The race leaders are coming already!" Little Dolphin clicked. He peered into the distance. "I can see Hamish – with Karen close behind! As soon as Vernon appears, we go into action!"

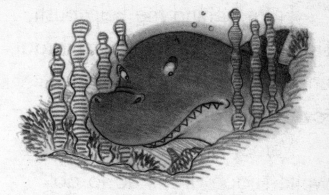

Vernon poked his head out, took one look at the racers and groaned. "Vinnie never said they'd be going *that* fast," he muttered. "Better get a move on!" And he shot out of the weeds towards Pebble Beach. "Trophy, here I come!" he called. "And with any luck I'll be taking it back to Shady Cove before Vinnie even knows who's won!"

From behind the kelp bush,
Little Dolphin watched as Fergal,
under the sail, slowly moved
towards Vernon.

Vernon spotted the eerie
white shape and tried to go

into reverse – but toppled over backwards on to the sea-bed. "It's a ghost!" he gulped as he lay floundering on the sand, eyes popping with fright.

Fergal loomed menacingly towards him, while Oscar made the horrible wailing sound. Before you could say 'shifty shark', Vernon shot back into the seaweed banks to hide!

A moment later, the race leaders sped by on their way to Pebble Beach.

"We've done it!" Little Dolphin whistled with relief. "Vernon will never catch them up now!"

"I don't think he'll ever come out of the seaweed!" joked Oscar, as the ghost floated back to them.

"That was brilliant, Fergal!" Little Dolphin whistled.

"Scary, you mean!" quavered Fergal from under the sail. "Can't stop my flippers from trembling!"

"It was those flippers that saved the race!" Little Dolphin chirped.

"The race!" cried Oscar. "We nearly forgot. You'd better get ready, Little Dolphin! Milo will be here any second."

Little Dolphin wasted no time.

He dashed out of the kelp bush –
and not a moment too soon!
There was Milo, racing towards
the seaweed banks! "Over here,
Milo!" he whistled.

Milo charged up to him.
"Good luck, Little Dolphin," he
gasped, as he slapped his
friend's flipper.

Little Dolphin set off as fast as he could. He couldn't believe it! He was taking part in the Great Underwater Race!

Soon the seaweed banks were far behind him as he sped along. He'd never swum so fast in his life. He flapped his tail hard and overtook three tiger fish and a porpoise. Ahead of him was a family of conger eels.

He leapt out of the water and jumped right over them. Then he dodged round a manta ray. Now he could hear the roar of the crowd as the winners crossed the finishing line.

Pebble Beach came into view at last! He wiggled his body and gave a final spurt forwards. He'd done it! There was his mum in the crowd, with a huge grin on her face – and Poppy's mum spinning madly next to her.

"Twenty-ninth!" Captain Capes called to Little Dolphin. "Well done, the dolphin team!"

Little Dolphin was very tired but also very happy.

Poppy and Hattie hurried over to him.

"Well done!" beamed Hattie. "I can't believe how fast you've all swum."

"Who won?" Little Dolphin asked.

"Hamish," Hattie told him, with a happy click of her claws.

"And there's no sign of those shifty sharks anywhere," chirped Poppy. "Your plan worked brilliantly, Little Dolphin!"

CHAPTER SIX

Everyone gathered round as Captain Capes presented the Great Underwater Race trophy. Little Dolphin, Poppy and Hattie waited at the back of the crowd. Oscar and Milo had joined them.

"Fergal will be along soon," Oscar told them. "He's a bit slow – he won't take his sail off!"

There was a hush as Captain
Capes held up the beautiful trophy.

Little Dolphin gazed at it
admiringly.

"And the winner of the Great
Underwater Race," announced
Captain Capes, "is Hamish!"

The crowd roared as Hamish
the hammerhead shark swam up
to collect his trophy.

"And I am delighted to
present an extra award," said
Captain Capes, when the
cheering had died down.
"An award for the youngest
swimmers ever to finish the
Great Underwater Race."

He held up three pieces of ribbon grass. Hanging from each one was a beautiful shiny shell medal. "Come forward, Little Dolphin, Milo and Poppy!"

The three friends stared at each other in amazement.

"Go on," said Hattie. "Don't keep the captain waiting."

The dolphin team swam shyly up to Captain Capes. Little Dolphin felt very proud as the captain placed a medal round his neck, and everyone cheered loudly.

As they made their way back into the crowd, they heard a voice behind them. It was Vinnie – and he was poking Vernon crossly with his nose.

"It's your fault we didn't win that trophy!" Vinnie growled. "If you saw a ghost, then I'm a sardine!"

"But there *was* a ghost!" whimpered Vernon. "It was huge and white and it howled horribly – and it quivered at me! I nearly died of shock!"

"There's no such things as ghosts, you cowardly cuttlefish," scoffed Vinnie.

"What's that over there, then?" quavered Vernon. A ghostly figure was floating along towards Pebble Beach.

Vinnie's mouth dropped open. "Save me, Vernon!" he wailed, diving behind his twin. "It's horrible!"

At that moment they saw Little Dolphin take the ghost in his teeth and give a tug. Fergal appeared with a shy smile.

"We've been tricked!" roared Vinnie. "That's not a ghost. It's just a turtle under a bit of sail!"

"That's cheating, that is!" growled Vernon. "He scared me on purpose and stopped *me* from cheating. I'm going to complain to Captain Capes."

"That's the most stupid idea you've ever had!" snapped Vinnie, slapping a flipper over his brother's mouth. "If you do that he'll know we were trying to cheat. You're coming with me before you get us both into trouble." And he dragged Vernon away by the tail.

Little Dolphin and his friends watched them go.

"I hope they've learnt their lesson," said Hattie firmly.

"I'm sure they have, coach," chuckled Oscar. "Thanks to our ghost here."

"Any time!" quavered Fergal.

"It's been a lovely day," sighed Poppy, spinning with happiness. "And tomorrow I'm going to make special medals for Fergal, Hattie and Oscar. We'd never have done so well without their help!"

"You'll be busy!" Little Dolphin said.

"Why's that?" asked Milo, puzzled.

"She'll have to make four for Fergal," Little Dolphin chirped. "One for each of his ghostly flippers!"